To

From

AUSTRALIA

Santa's Aussie Holiday

For Max, Sam, Marissa, Lotte and Lilly   MF

For Olive, Joseph and Sam   AW

Scholastic Press
345 Pacific Highway
Lindfield NSW 2070
An imprint of Scholastic Australia Pty Limited (ABN 11 000 614 577)
PO Box 579 Gosford NSW 2250
www.scholastic.com.au

Part of the Scholastic Group
Sydney • Auckland • New York • Toronto • London • Mexico City
• New Delhi • Hong Kong • Buenos Aires • Puerto Rico

First published by Scholastic Australia in 2007.
Text copyright © Maria Farrer, 2007.
Illustrations copyright © Anna Walker, 2007.

Rock paintings inspired by the art of Injalak Hill, Gunbalanya (Oenpelli),
Northern Territory.

National Library of Australia Cataloguing-in-Publication entry
Farrer, Maria, 1962- .
    Santa's Aussie holiday.
    For children.
    ISBN 9781741690187 (hbk.).
    1. Santa Claus - Juvenile fiction. 2. Holidays - Australia
    - Juvenile fiction. 3. Christmas stories, Australian.
    4. Australia - Juvenile fiction. I. Walker, Anna. II. Title.
NZ823.3

Typeset in Athenaeum.

Printed by Tien Wah Press, Malaysia.

10 9 8 7 6 5 4 3 2   7 8 9 / 0

Santa's Aussie Holiday

Maria Farrer   Anna Walker

A Scholastic Press book from Scholastic Australia

The Arctic's cold, with ice and snow,
and that's where Santa lives, you know.

On Christmas Eve he flies so fast
we rarely see him whizzing past—
but he keeps a lookout on his way
for a place to take his holiday.

Each year he likes to have some fun,
a chance to get some rest and sun;
he spins his globe for inspiration
and finds a perfect destination.

A big smile spreads across his face . . .

Australia is the perfect place!

He packs his bag, his surfboard too,
and lands his sleigh at Australia Zoo.
He leaves his reindeer in the care
of friendly locals who live there.

He hires a ute and takes a ride
to town—to buy a tourist guide,
a T-shirt, thongs and bushman's hat,
stubbies—and Aussie things like that.

He heads to Fraser Island first,
the heat, it gives him quite a thirst!
He cools off in the champagne pools
and learns about the dingo rules.

And after going four-wheel driving,
he heads up north for scuba diving.
He dives around the Barrier Reef
and meets a shark with long sharp teeth!

He drives across the desert sands
to where magnificent Uluru stands
and watches till the day is through,
then leaves to visit . . .

Kakadu.

The crocodiles, they make him shiver
as he cruises up the yellow river;
but the ancient art of the Aboriginal
he finds both interesting and original.

In Albany he watches whales
and walks along the forest trails.
He meets the quokkas on Rottnest
before he turns to leave the west.

On Phillip Island, just by chance,
he joins in the koala dance.
And as the sun sets, gold and red,
the fairy penguins come home to bed.

Tasmania next—where he finds a spot,
as crew upon a racing yacht.
The wind is strong, the sea is rough,
soon Santa thinks he's had enough!

But in Sydney there is much to do:
a skywalk, cruise and opera too.
And though the Harbour Bridge is high,
Santa climbs it—what a guy!

His speedos (red and white and tight)
give Bondi surfies quite a fright.
The big waves leave him feeling dizzy;
he keeps the lifeguards very busy!

Although he's having so much fun
on holiday in the sea and sun,
he knows he has to head back north,
to prepare for December 24th.

He hangs a boomerang on his sleigh,
shouts, 'See ya mate' and is on his way.
And though he's very sad to leave,
he'll be back in Oz on Christmas Eve.